the alphabet tree

leo lionni

the alphabet tree

Leo Lionni

Alfred A. Knopf · New York

THIS IS A BORZOI BOOK PUBLISHED BY ALFRED A. KNOPF

Copyright © 1968, renewed 1996 by Leo Lionni

All rights reserved under International and Pan-American Copyright Conventions. Published
in the United States by Alfred A. Knopf, an imprint of Random House Children's Books, a
division of Random House, Inc., New York, and simultaneously in Canada by Random House
of Canada Limited, Toronto. Distributed by Random House, Inc., New York. Originally
published by Pantheon, a division of Random House, Inc., in 1968.

KNOPF, BORZOI BOOKS, and the colophon are registered trademarks of Random House, Inc.

Library of Congress Cataloging-in-Publication Data

Lionni, Leo, 1910–1999 The alphabet tree / Leo Lionni. p. cm.

SUMMARY: After a storm blows some of them away, the letters on the alphabet tree learn from a strange bug to be stronger by forming words.
Then a caterpillar comes along and tells them that words are not enough; they must say something important.

ISBN 0-394-81016-3 (trade) — ISBN 0-394-91016-8 (lib. bdg.) — ISBN 0-679-80835-3 (pbk.)

[1. Alphabet—Fiction. 2. Writing—Fiction. 3. Insects—Fiction. 4. Caterpillars—Fiction.] I. Title. PZ7.L6634Al 2004   [E]—dc22   2003016215

www.randomhouse.com/kids   MANUFACTURED IN MALAYSIA   June 2004   15 14 13 12 11 10 9 8 7 6

"This is the Alphabet Tree," said the ant.
"Why is it called the Alphabet Tree?" asked
his friend.

"Because not so long ago this tree was full of letters. They lived a happy life, hopping from leaf to leaf on the highest twigs.

Each letter had its favorite leaf, where it would sit in the sun and rock in the gentle breeze of spring.

One day the breeze became a strong gust and the gust became a gale.

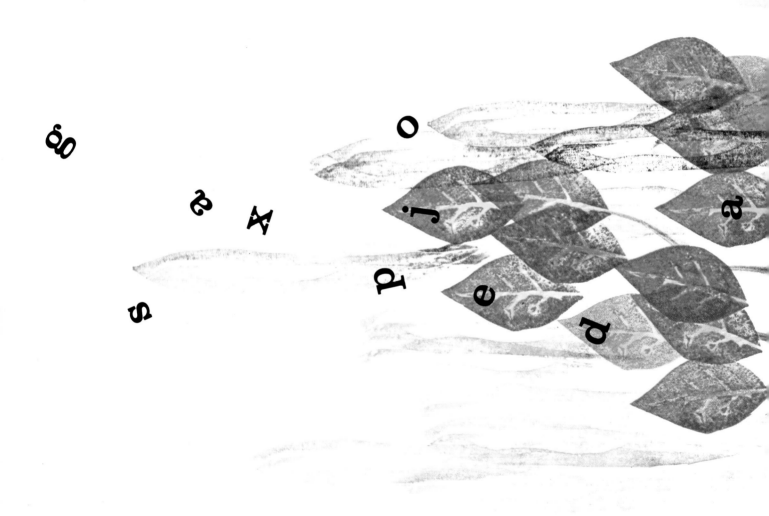

The letters clung to the leaves with all their might—but some were
blown away, and the others were very frightened.

When the storm had passed they huddled together in fear, deep in the foliage of the lower branches.

A funny bug, red and black with
bright yellow wings, saw them there,
hiding in the shade.
'We are hiding from the wind,'
the letters explained. 'But who are you?'
'I am the word-bug,' the bug answered.
'I can teach you to make words.
If you get together in threes and fours,
and even more,
no wind will be strong enough
to blow you away.'

z

cat

bug leaf y

we

tree s

d me

o

i e c

n

u p

u

Patiently he taught the letters to join together and make words.

cat

leaf

red

bug

tree

we

you

zoo

small

earth

big

peace

now

men

Some made short and easy words like *dog* and *cat*, others learned to make more difficult ones: *twig*, *leaf*, and even *earth*.

A

twig

wind

green

Happily they climbed back onto the highest leaves, and when the wind came they held on without fear. The word-bug had been right.

peace

on good

tree

men and

red will

earth

Then, one summer morning, a strange caterpillar appeared amid the foliage. He was purple, woolly, and very large. 'Such confusion!' said the caterpillar when he saw the words scattered around the leaves. 'Why don't you get together and make sentences—and *mean* something?'

cat

on

red

ea

men

tree

ill

small

peace

green

and

to

leaf

The letters had never thought of this. Now they could really write—*say* things. They said things about the wind, the leaves, the bug. 'Good!' said the caterpillar approvingly. 'But not good enough.'

the wind is bad

leaves are green

the bug is small

'Why?' asked the letters, surprised.
'Because you must say something *important*,'
said the caterpillar.

peace on earth and

The letters tried to think of something important, *really* important. Finally they knew what to say. What could be more important than peace? PEACE ON EARTH AND GOODWILL TOWARD ALL MEN, they spelled excitedly.

will toward all men

'Great!' said the caterpillar. 'Now climb onto my back.' One by one the letters climbed onto the woolly back. 'But where are you taking us?' they asked anxiously, as the caterpillar began climbing down the tree.

'To the President,' said the caterpillar.''

peace